PRESENTED TO

....

FROM

....

DATE

....

A Hat for Ivan

Max Lucado

Illustrated by David Wenzel

CROSSWAY BOOKS · WHEATON, ILLINOIS

A DIVISION OF GOOD NEWS PUBLISHERS

JE
LUC

A Hat for Ivan
Text copyright © 2004 by Max Lucado
Illustrations © 2004 by David Wenzel

www.ahatforivan.com

Published by Crossway Books
a division of Good News Publishers
1300 Crescent Street
Wheaton, Illinois 60187

Edited by Karen Hill
Design: David Uttley, UDG | DesignWorks, www.udgdesignworks.com
First printing 2004
Printed in the United States of America

LIBRARY OF CONGRESS CATALOGING-IN-PUBLICATION DATA

Lucado, Max.
  A hat for Ivan / Max Lucado ; illustrated by David Wenzel.
      p. cm.
Summary: On Hat Day, Ivan expects his father, the hat-maker, to present him with a hat that matches his character and talents, but he becomes confused when the other villagers also give him headgear more appropriate to their own interests.
  ISBN 1-58134-414-7 (HC : alk. paper)
  [1. Identity--Fiction. 2. Hats--Fiction. 3. Fathers and sons--Fiction.] I. Wenzel, David, 1950- ill. II. Title.
PZ7.L9684Hat 2004
[E]--dc22
                                    2003019027

LB 12 11 10 09 08 07 06 05 04
15 14 13 12 11 10 9 8 7 6 5 4 3 2 1

FOR ART MILLER

Thanks for helping me (and millions of others)
wear the hat the Father intended.

A Hat  for Ivan

Ivan was a happy boy.

He lived in the town of Hatville, a place where everyone wore hats.

Not just any hats. The doctors wore doctor hats. The cooks wore cooking hats. The farmers wore farming hats. Everyone wore hats and . . .

Ivan's father was the hat-maker. A very good hat-maker. Ivan loved to watch him work. People would come to his shop to order a hat, and Ivan's father would ask, "What do you really love to do?"

"I love to fish," one man said.

"Do you fish well?"

"That I do!"

"Then you need a fishing hat."

And so Ivan's father would make it—complete with a pocket for the hooks and a small bucket for the bait. He made everyone a hat. And since everyone wore a hat, everyone knew what everyone else loved to do and did well.

A Hat  for Ivan

Want some flowers? Talk to the lady with the roses on her head. Need directions? Ask the man with a hat made from a map. Wondering how to fix a fence? Look for the fellow who wears a hat shaped like a hammer.

Everyone wore hats, and Ivan's dad made hats.

Could anything be better than that? One thing could. Getting your own hat.

And Ivan was about to receive his. At the age of ten each boy and girl celebrated Hat Day. Ivan was nine, going on ten. He could hardly wait to get his hat.

What will mine look like? he wondered. Would it be made of felt like the clerks'? Bright blue like the policemen's? Covered with cloth like the dressmakers'?

He didn't know. But he would find out soon.

All Ivan could think about was his new hat. All he could talk about was his new hat. He told everyone he saw, "My Hat Day is coming!"

A Hat  for Ivan

The people in Hatville were excited for Ivan. Some people had their own ideas about what kind of hat he should wear.

Felix the baker did. Ivan passed Felix's bakery every morning on the way to school. And every morning Ivan stopped in the doorway and smelled the baking bread. He couldn't always see Felix (Felix was short and round like the cookies he baked), but he could always see Felix's bobbing hat.

It was tall and white like the wedding cakes he made.

One day when Ivan stopped by for a sniff, Felix was waiting for him. "I hear you are about to get your hat." He smiled at the young boy.

"I am," Ivan replied with pride.

"Well, I have a surprise for you. Come in."

And with that, the baker stepped back into the shop, and Ivan followed. What could the surprise be? A doughnut? Some cookie dough?

A Hat  for Ivan

No. Felix didn't give Ivan something to eat. He gave him something to wear. "I have a hat for you!" announced the baker.

Ivan was surprised. Not disappointed. Not happy. Just surprised. He thought his hat would come from his father, the hat-maker. But, then again, maybe he was wrong. Besides, Ivan didn't want to hurt his friend's feelings.

"Thank you, Mr. Felix," Ivan said, taking the hat.

"Go ahead, put it on."

And so Ivan did. But it was too big. It fell, not just over his eyes—but over his whole face.

"That's okay, little friend. It will soon fit. Just wear it anyway."

Ivan didn't know what to say except, "Thanks again." And he turned to walk out the door. But when he did, he ran into the wall.

"Here, I'll help you," offered Felix, guiding his friend to the door. "You look great, just like me."

Ivan started to say thanks again, but he tripped on the step and fell flat on his back. "Funny," he said to himself, "I thought my hat would fit better than this."

A Hat  for Ivan

Since he walked the same path to school every morning, Ivan was able to feel his way down the street. Soon the scent of daisies and roses told him he was nearing the flower shop. When he heard the hammers pounding, he knew he was near the carpenter's shop. And the sound of music told him he was passing by Miss Anita's piano studio.

Miss Anita loved music. And Miss Anita loved Ivan. Ivan's father had made her a special music hat—wide, round with tiny guitars on top, and piano strings dangling from the brim. Since each string had a bell on the end, everyone knew when Miss Anita was near.

It was a different sort of hat, but it was perfect for Miss Anita. No one else would want to wear it, but Miss Anita wouldn't be without it. She loved the hat, and she loved Ivan. And she loved it when he stopped to hear her play.

Of course, on this day, she didn't recognize him.

All she saw was a tall hat on a small boy.

"Who are you?" she asked.

From within the hat came a muffled voice. "It's me, Miss Anita. It's Ivan."

He heard her quick steps on the wooden floor. "That's not the hat for you," she declared as she yanked it off his head.

A Hat for Ivan

"It's not?" he replied.

"Of course not! There is only one hat for you." Suddenly Miss Anita disappeared into her studio and came out with a very different-looking hat.

"I made this just for you. I've been working on it for days. Here, try it on."

Ivan was surprised. Not happy. Not disappointed. Just surprised. He'd never seen a hat like this one. "Funny," Ivan said to himself, "Miss Anita is a good musician, but she's not a good hat-maker."

A piccolo dangled from the side, and sheet music was glued to the top. Bells and whistles hung in front of Ivan's face, and a drumstick dangled like a ponytail on his back.

"It looks perfect," Miss Anita declared. "This hat was made for you."

Ivan smiled. The music teacher turned and walked back into the studio, pleased with herself. Now Ivan had two hats. One in his hand and one on his head. He didn't like wearing either one, but he did not want to hurt anyone's feelings.

He didn't know what else to do except keep walking to school. But the hat-maker's son was barely down the street when he met a new problem.

A Hat  for Ivan

"Ivan!" The voice was deep and big and belonged to Bruno the firefighter. "What is that on your head?"

"Miss Anita gave it to me."

"As a joke?"

"No, for real."

"It's a good thing I came along. I knew your Hat Day was near; so I brought you a gift."

For the third time that day, a hat was placed on Ivan's head.

This hat was just like Bruno's—long and red and very shiny.

A piece of fire hose was wrapped around it, and a miniature ladder stood straight up on top. The big fireman held the hat steady while Ivan tightened the strap beneath his chin.

A Hat  for Ivan

"Now that is what I call a hat," Bruno boomed in his deep voice. Ivan stepped back, and when he did, he fell over. The hat was so tall and heavy that the boy couldn't keep his balance. Bruno helped him up, stepped back, and Ivan fell again.

"You'll get used to it, Ivan," Bruno told him. "I did." And with that he turned to leave.

Ivan tried and tried to stand but kept falling backwards. He stepped back as fast as he could until his back was against a wall. "Thanks, Mr. Bruno," he shouted, although he didn't feel thankful. *Funny,* Ivan thought to himself, *it's easy for Bruno to wear this big hat but hard for me.*

What he did feel was confused. When he had left the house, he had no hats. Now he had three, and he didn't like any of them. With one he couldn't see. With the other he didn't want to be seen, and with the third he couldn't stand up.

What was he going to do?

He did not know what to do except to go on to school. So with one hand holding the heavy hat on his head and one hand holding the others, he carefully walked the rest of the way.

A Hat  for Ivan

Things didn't get any better at school; in fact, they got worse. His hats interrupted the class. If he wore the baker's hat, everyone chuckled. If he wore the musical hat, he made too much noise. He tried to keep Bruno's hat on his head, but he kept falling off his chair.

"Ivan," the teacher finally decided, "maybe you better go home."

Ivan was sad, but he knew she was right. He still didn't know what to do.

He had too many hats!

And on the way home, he was given many more. The farmer gave him a straw hat with a bandanna—to keep the sun off. The beekeeper gave him a netted one—to keep the bees out. The woodsman gave him a wool cap— to keep his ears warm. A clown gave him a cone hat with many colors. And the bookshop owner gave him a hat shaped like a dictionary.

A Hat  for Ivan

Ivan soon had so many hats that he could barely carry them all. He would drop one, and when he bent over to pick it up, he would drop another. He finally had them balanced when, all of a sudden, he saw Felix the baker. *Oh, no,* he thought, *I'm wearing the farmer's hat.* So he dropped them all and just barely got the baker's hat on his head—and over his eyes—when Felix saw him.

"Looks great, Ivan!" shouted Felix.

Ivan sounded tired. "Thanks."

Balancing the hats was hard enough, but now Ivan's eyes were covered as he walked.

He couldn't see where he was going. He had stopped to rest when he heard the tinkling of tiny bells. It was Miss Anita!

A Hat for Ivan

Ivan pulled off the baker hat and threw on the musical hat just in time. "Oh, you look wonderful!" Miss Anita exclaimed as she passed.

Ivan had started picking up the rest of the hats when he heard the deep voice of Bruno. "Ivan, is that you?"

As quickly as he could, Ivan replaced the musical hat with the firefighter's hat. "It's me," he said, straightening, then falling back and back and back until he landed on his bottom.

Bruno didn't see Ivan fall; he was already turning the corner.

"Looks terrific, my friend," Bruno called over his shoulder.

"Thanks," Ivan mumbled to no one but himself. He was so tired he didn't even try to get up. He just sat there, surrounded by hats.

"Looks like you've had quite a day."

Ivan couldn't remember when a voice ever sounded so good.

"Father!" he shouted, jumping up. "You won't believe what happened today. Everybody gave me a hat and—"

"None of them fit?" Ivan's father spoke up.

"That's right," said the boy.

"And they make you tired?"

Ivan nodded.

"But you don't want to hurt anyone's feelings?"

Ivan shook his head.

His father put his arm around his son.

"That's right." Ivan stopped. "How did you know?"

"I'm the hat-maker, Ivan. I have seen what happens when people wear hats they weren't intended to wear. They feel silly. They fall down. And they get tired."

Ivan's father got down on his knees and wiped a smudge of dirt off his son's cheek.

"Listen, son, just because someone gives you a hat, that doesn't mean you are supposed to wear it. They mean well, but they don't know you. That's my job. I'm the hat-maker, and I'm your father."

"So you'll make a hat just for me?"

"I will. All you have to do is ask."

"Oh, please, Father." Ivan smiled. "I would like that very much."

"Well, let's gather up these hats and go home then."

As the hat-maker and his child walked toward home, the father asked, "Tell me, Ivan, what do you really love to do?"

OTHER CROSSWAY BOOKS
BY MAX LUCADO

All You Ever Need

Because I Love You

Best of All

If Only I Had a Green Nose

Just the Way You Are

Tell Me the Secrets

Tell Me the Story

With You All the Way

Resurrection Morning

You Are Mine

You Are Special